This Bing book belongs to:

....

Copyright © 2019 Acamar Films Ltd

The Bing television series is created by Acamar Films and Brown Bag Films and adapted from the original books by Ted Dewan

Based on the episode *Woof!* by Lead Writer Helen Farrall and Team Writers Lucy Murphy, Mikael Shields and An Vrombaut

Edited by Emma Drage
Designed by Candice Turvey and Wayne Redwood

First published in Great Britian in 2018 by HarperCollins *Children's Books*.
HarperCollins *Children's Books* is a division of HarperCollins *Publishers* Ltd, 1 London Bridge Street, London, SE1 9GF
HarperCollins*Publishers* Macken House, 39/40 Mayor Street Upper Dublin 1, D01 C9W8, Ireland

3 5 7 9 10 8 6 4

978-0-00-797950-9

Printed in China

MIX
Paper from
responsible sources
FSC C007454

Hello Doggy!

HarperCollins *Children's Books*

Round the corner, not far
away, Bing and Flop are
going to the park today.

Bing and Flop play with the ball.

Hup!

Hup!

Oops!

Bing throws the ball **really** far.

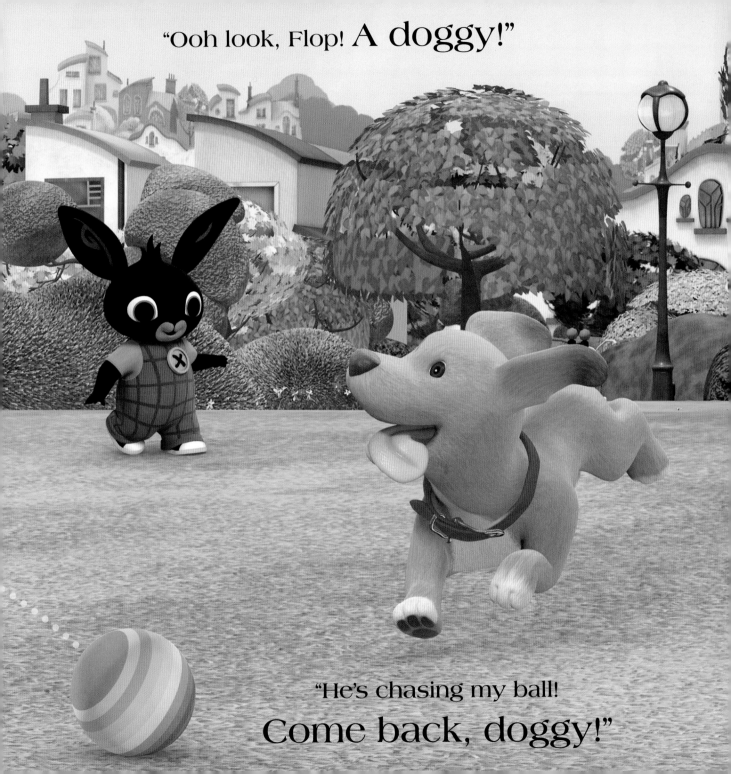

"Ooh look, Flop! A doggy!"

"He's chasing my ball!
Come back, doggy!"

"Hello, Doggy!"

Bing wants to play with the dog.

Flop shows Bing how to make friends with the dog.

"We need to be nice and quiet. Then you hold your hand out low so the dog can smell you."

"There we are. Now, you come and make friends too, Bing."

Hello, doggy!

"He's wagging his tail!"

"I think he likes you, Bing."

"Good doggy," says Bing, gently stroking the dog. "What's your name?"

Flop looks at
the dog's collar.
"Hmm...there's
no name tag."

Woof!

"Can we keep him?" asks Bing.

"Sorry, Bing. We can't keep him, but we can look after him until his owner comes back."

The ball lands behind a bush.

"What's the doggy doing?" asks Bing.

"I think he's going to smell
where the ball went," says Flop.

Flop puts the poo
in a special poo bin.

"When you have a dog,
you have to do the
yucky stuff as well
as the fun stuff, Bing."

"We'll need to wash
our hands when we
get home."

"But not in
the park!"

The dog gives Bing a playful lick.
"Aww...he LOVES me, Flop!"

"Yes, he does."

"Can we keep him **NOW**, Flop?"

"Sorry, Bing, we still can't keep him. He's not ours."

"**Oh**, but he's my friend," says Bing sadly.

Bing!
Flop!

"Look!" says Flop. "It's Gilly and Popsie."

"Hello, Bing. Oh, you've found Sunshine. Thank you for looking after her."

"Oh! Sunshine is a girl dog," says Bing.

Woof!

Woof!

"Yes, she's Popsie's sister," says Gilly.

"And she's my friend," says Bing.

"Yes, I can see she really likes you, Bing.
Would you like to play with her next week?"

"Ooh! Yes, please!"

"Time to go home now, Sunshine.
Bing, would you like to hold her lead?"

Hi!

I saw a **doggy** in the park. She's called **Sunshine**.

You have to let a doggy **smell you** to make friends, and then you can play catch together.

Woof!

I wanted to keep the doggy. But Flop said we couldn't because she's not ours, and then I was sad.

Oh!

But then Gilly came and said I can play with her next week because she's my new friend.

Dogs…

they're a Bing thing.